Spoil the Child

by

Denise Howard Long

Finishing Line Press
Georgetown, Kentucky

Spoil the Child

ACKNOWLEDGMENTS

Credits
Some of these stories appeared, sometimes in different form, in the following
publications:

"What We See," *The Tishman Review* and *Best Small Fictions 2018*
"A Smooth, Shallow Cut," *Smokelong Quarterly*
"Carnival Ride," *Pank*
"In the Front Room, In the Kitchen" and "Where Nobody Might See,"
Evansville Review
"Who's There," *Kentucky Review*
"Taxidermy," *Crack the Spine*
"Block Party Games," *Foliate Oak Magazine*
"Dollhouse," *Journal of the Compressed Creative Arts*
"Summer's End," *The Alchemist Review* and *The Story Shack*

Publisher: Leah Maines
Editor: Christen Kincaid
Cover Art: Peter Heeling/Skitterphoto
Author Photo: Nellie Smith
Cover Design: Elizabeth Maines McCleavy

Printed in the USA on acid-free paper.
Order online: www.finishinglinepress.com
              also available on amazon.com

Author inquiries and mail orders:
Finishing Line Press
P. O. Box 1626
Georgetown, Kentucky 40324
U. S. A.

Table of Contents

A Smooth, Shallow Cut

Hadley knew she wasn't supposed to be out there. But nobody had said much of anything about what she did or didn't do for quite some time, certainly not since her mother left forty-two days ago. The night was quiet. The low hum of staticky country and western music floated across the garage, eclipsed every now and then by the harsh electric of the bug zapper down by the burn barrel. From where she stood just outside the door, her father couldn't see her unless he was looking. The thick red vinyl cord was looped around the deer's neck and then draped over the hoist in the garage. Hadley considered making herself known, offering herself up, showing she wasn't afraid. But she stayed where she was, watching the deer's long limbs stretch endlessly toward the concrete floor.

She breathed heavily out, expecting to see her breath on the night air, but nothing came out. Cold, but not that cold. Her father coughed and she startled, her eyes catching on the hunting knife on the counter—out of its case and lying crooked like it had been tossed, rather than set down gently, the way a knife that big should. If she rocked back and forth on her toes, the edge of the blade reflected the humming fluorescent light that hung from the ceiling. Everything looked too sharp to be real.

She watched the rough flannel of her father's plaid shirt stretch tight as he leaned over in the corner, his hands working at something she couldn't see. She caught sight of the lighter in his hand and a charred smell filled the air. The hum of his breath sucking in reminded her of his body stretched out on the couch, his head rolled back in sleep, whiskered throat flung up toward the ceiling. A tired sort of violence would fill the room along with the vibrations of his snores, and time would stretch out in anticipation of when he would wake.

She wondered if the deer had heard him coming. If it had seen her father and his gun and known to be afraid. In her mind, she pictured the deer stepping toward her father, full of curiosity and wonder, with no idea what the next moments would bring.

Hadley imagined the hunting knife touching the deer's skin and then thought of it touching her own. She wondered if it would throb, like the toothache she'd had last spring. The one that felt like a pulse in her mouth that woke her in the night and kept her from eating for days.

Or maybe the knife on her skin would feel like when she'd stepped in a yellow jacket nest by the creek. She'd hopped in the water to soothe the sting, the cold water numbing her skin. She'd stood there for ages, knowing when she stepped out the bite of pain would return. She wondered if wetting the deer before her father made his cuts would help, although she supposed it didn't really matter anymore now.

She knew enough to know that her father would first make a smooth, shallow cut to peel back the skin, keeping the coarse brown hair from the meat. She knew that the second cut would go deep enough to empty the deer, the blade moving from end to end, opening the animal wide. The metal tub on the stained concrete beneath would catch what fell out. She imagined how light the deer would feel once it had lost everything inside.

Who's There

When we make our nighttime trips across town, Mom lets me sit in the front seat on the way there, instead of buckled in back. The car glides out of our neighborhood and onto the highway. The street lights shine through the windshield and I watch the dashboard go from light to dark, light to dark.

The air is thick. Mom hasn't said a word since she woke me up.

"Are you sure Dad's there?"

She nods.

"Do I have to go to the door?"

"We'll just wait and see."

Our tires crunch on rocks in the driveway. In the quiet, every sound shatters.

Mom sighs.

The porch light is on. That means I need to go up.

"I guess I'll be right back," I say. She stares straight ahead, motionless.

I nod for no particular reason and open the car door.

I reach the front door of the house, and my gut churns. I knock and wait. I know who will answer and it won't be my dad.

Jane cracks the door and a sly grin spreads her lips, smudged and red. Her long bright nails click on the edge of the door. "Hey there, Sebaaaaastian," she purrs.

I choke down the bitter taste rising in my throat.

She leans back from the door and into her house, and I hear her call my dad's name.

"Da-an!" Extra A's in his name too. "Guess who's here." She laughs and sways, her shiny robe barely to her knees. The fabric belt dangles down her pale legs. She steps toward the porch and I move out of her way. I follow her gaze to the car, but all I can see is the back of Mom's head because she's turned away.

Jane's hand reaches out to stroke my hair, but I twist my head and look at the ground.

"She ain't all there, huh?" she hisses. "I mean why else would she keep at it? I know she's your mama, but she's just not all there."

My throat tightens and I shrug.

"She knows. Hell, half the town knows. But she doesn't do a damn thing different. And then she makes you come up while she sits and waits? You know it's not his fault, right? If she were a better wife, he wouldn't do this. You know that, right?"

All her sentences sound like questions, but she doesn't wait for answers.

She's saying more to me than anyone has all week, and part of me wants to say something back. To say something to wipe the smugness from her face. But I have no idea what words that would be. I never know the right things to say, to do.

Every day, I sit alone at lunch, in the loud hum of the cafeteria. Everyone else talks and trades food. But not me. On the bus, I don't sit alone. My neighborhood is full of bus kids, so there's always two or three to a seat. Some days, I sit on the floor in the aisle. It's just easier to stay down when the other kids have pushed me there.

I don't mention any of this at home. I don't tell my mom about the way kids sometimes throw wet scraps of paper in my hair. I keep silent about the way I'm always picked last in PE. And I never tell her about how my teachers look at me like I'm something caught behind glass. How, when our eyes meet, their lips go thin and their eyes shift anywhere else. It's only nice to watch something trapped when it doesn't see you watching.

My hands ache and I realize my nails are digging into the palms of my hands. I stretch out my fingers and stare at the half-moons dug into my skin. I feel the blood pulsing just beneath the surface, where I can't reach it.

My dad's heavy footfalls stomp down the stairs inside. The door opens wide as he leans back and groans. He takes a swig from his can, crunches it between his fingers, and drops it near a box by the door. His belch echoes against the metal porch awning and the hairs on the back of my neck stiffen.

"Well, Jane, I gotta go. My chariot awaits." He gives a sweeping bow and laughs, the sound rough on my ears.

I turn my head as he leans to kiss her. I hope his lips find her cheek, the top of her head, the back of a hand, but I hear the sound of his mouth on hers.

I think of how my mom used to kiss me good-night. How my dad used to be there too. Back before the union contract was up. Back before he spat about "filthy scabs" and not "giving a shit" what she "heard on the news." I think of the yelling and slamming doors and how their fights created a heat that seemed to come through the walls and into my room. How my mom would come to my bed at night, crying and apologizing for what I had heard.

In time, the fights cooled. My mom's yelling and crying turned into nodding and hand wringing. Everything in the house went cold and quiet, and I couldn't decide if the before or the after was closer to normal. I couldn't decide what I wanted them to be.

As I heard my dad's lips linger on Jane's mouth, a giggle in her throat,

I gritted myself and squeezed my eyes shut. I turned my head toward the driveway and willed it to be empty. For Mom to have backed the car out silently, turned down the street and driven away. Away from all this, even if she'd left me behind.

But she's looking right at me. Her lips a hard line that has almost disappeared. She nods tightly, and in the space from her to me, I feel the gathering weight of our shame.

What We See

The baby began walking just a few months after being born, proving she was just as exceptional as we had planned her to be. But she refused to walk during the day. Only at night. When we were asleep.

At first I wasn't certain what was going on; I only knew that in the morning something felt different. A shift as subtle as the temperature dipping or the wind gently shifting its direction. A feeling that, in some ways, only a mother would know.

But, in time, my husband sensed it too. Then he'd ask if I was feeling all right, ask if I also felt something was off, some indescribable thing different from before.

Before what, I had asked, still trying to piece it together myself. He'd shrugged and assured me it was probably nothing.

And we'd check on our sleeping baby before he'd scuttle off to work.

There she was, asleep in her crib, pacifier tucked between her lips. Always her arms flung to her sides, as if she'd fallen to the mattress from a great height. But as I lay my hand upon her chest, feeling the rise and fall of her breaths, I noticed the blackened bottoms of her footie pajamas. I knew without doubt she'd been up to something while we slept.

And then there were the more obvious traces she began to leave behind.

Dishes my husband had left on the counter were suddenly now washed and put away. But they were in the cabinets upside down, stacked in precarious sculptures prepared to fall when I opened the door.

My toothbrush would be pulled from its cup, resting on the counter, sticky globs of pale blue toothpaste clinging to the bristles and dripping down the side—one more thing for me to scrub.

At first, my husband laughed and thought I was joking. But I showed him the pajamas, the dishes, reminded him of the morning air that had felt different for days. I thought he would laugh, tell me I was crazy, but he didn't. He thought it was cute. These little things that would happen while we slept. He marveled at her cleverness and ingenuity and told me *that's our girl.*

I'd smiled and agreed that *yes, she most certainly was.*

And each day we'd awaken, ready for what new trail she'd leave behind.

***

One morning the garage door was left open, the engine running in one of the cars. My husband swore he hadn't left keys in the ignition this time.

And the baby still refused to walk during the day. She was sitting up easily now. And sometimes she would stand, gurgles of baby drool clinging to her lips. But just in that moment we were prepared for her to move, she'd collapse back down, her ripe diaper hitting the carpet like soured fruit.

I'd watch my husband to see if he noticed her smirk like I did. And he'd sigh and ask me again what she and I did all day, what it was I was missing that I should somehow see.

He thought if we could make the baby stop walking at night, she'd have to walk in the day. We could record videos of her toddling, one foot in front of the other, posting them online for the entire world to see, sharing her in a way we'd avoided because our secret was too strange to believe.

The first attempt was putting the baby gate across her bedroom door at night. But in the morning, the gate was folded neatly in the hall.

We tried staying up all night, waiting. But my husband could never seem to stay awake during his turn to watch.

We set up a camera in her room to catch her in the act but no matter how we placed it, the angle was never quite right.

Each night, we'd creep into her room on our way to bed and we'd watch her sleep. Lingering, I'd become lost in the idea that she had no idea I was there, standing right on the lavender rug that I'd selected over a year earlier. She slept on, as if my presence didn't matter at all.

***

The air in our house had become stifling, a dense, warm sensation filling us both with the unknown that we were desperate to know. I could see it in my husband's eyes, the fear of what we needed to witness but hadn't yet figured out how. A feeling of unease grew deep in my body, my feet always heavy.

I mentioned perhaps putting a lock on her door, from the outside, the idea giving way in my mind like rocks knocked loose by rushing water.

But what about a fire? my husband said. *She wouldn't be able to get out.*

Later, he would deny it had been his idea.

What we both agreed to was intended to be a small kitchen fire. A few splashes of gasoline and the flick of a match. Just enough that the baby would smell the smoke and walk out. And we'd see her. We'd see her coming outside, walking, and it would be night but we would see.

And as we stood on the lawn, watching the flames climb higher and higher, my husband pulled away, moved toward the house. And I dug my nails into his arm and said, *Wait. Just a little bit more. I still want to see.*

Carnival Ride

Tommy's hand had just slid under the hem of my skirt when the Ferris wheel shuddered to a halt. The screech of metal pierced my brain and I resisted the urge to slap Tommy's hand away.

We were at the very top and I looked down across the entire town square. Across the midway, I could hear kids screaming as the Salt and Pepper Shakers flung them. I imagined how blurry everything would look as the little cages shook them up and down. The other direction, I could see the yellow and white striped beer tent, the bass of a local band thumping from inside.

Just past the square, I could see the middle school where I'd start eighth grade in just two weeks. And if I leaned way forward, I'd see down onto the ground, where Billy and Ricky were waiting for their turn to ride. I thought of the carnie who'd pulled down the metal bar to our laps, how he'd eyed Tommy and smirked at me, the words *Like mother, like daughter* sitting just behind his teeth.

At first I thought the stop was because they were offloading other people, which would be strange because we'd been the last ones on. But a ride cut short didn't seem to be stopping Tommy's stride. His fingers had already found their way to the seam of my underpants and his breath quickened against my neck. I wondered if he thought about kissing me. If he wanted to or not.

"Wonder if someone puked," he whispered after some time had passed and the wheel still hadn't moved. His face burrowed into my shoulder as his fingers pushed and pulled like he was searching for something to pull out of me.

"Nobody throws up on the Ferris wheel."

***

Last year at Frontier Days, they had to shut the wheel down. A little girl had fallen from the top. The carnival had continued, but barricades and tape had marked the spot where she'd landed until days later when the rides and tents left town.

She'd been tucked in next to her dad, her little sister on his other side, but the safety bar popped loose. People said the seat had suddenly lurched forward, and the man had grabbed one of them just as the other fell.

The morning after it happened, my mother told me the story in vivid detail—the father's screams, the impossible angle of the little girl's neck—though I knew she'd not actually seen it. Her voice was like gravel as she tapped cigarette ashes in the sink and I waited for breakfast.

"But where was that girl's momma is what I'd like to know. Mothers don't let things like that happen."

And I'd swallowed my juice as I watched her slide a knife through her beer tent wristband from the night before, letting the green neon plastic join the ashes in the sink before she went back to smearing butter on blackened toast.

I hadn't thought about the girl's mother, though. Or even the baby who'd lost her sister in such a gruesome way. Instead, I thought about the girl's dad and wondered if he hated himself. If he would wake up every morning for the rest of his life wondering if he'd saved the wrong one. If he replayed that moment, picturing how he could have done something different and what that might have meant. If maybe some morning he'd just leave it all and not look back, knowing that sometimes your choices just aren't your own.

***

When the Ferris wheel finally shook free and we started to move again, I thought about pushing the bar up from our laps. For just a second, I thought of how it would feel to dive toward the ground and never feel the landing. Instead, I let my legs fall open for Tommy, waited for my stomach to drop, and pretended I was anywhere but where I was.

Heavy

None of us saw it coming when Randall jumped in the water. We didn't even know if he could swim. Randall had refused to get in the pool all summer. It wasn't until the third week of camp that Robby, our counselor, convinced him to put on swim trunks. They were neon orange and the pale ripple of his stomach hung in exhaustion over his waistband. And we'd snickered as he sat on one of the flowered chairs near the shallow end and never came close to where we were. He never got in the water at all.

Until he did.

The day he jumped, we'd canoed out to the lagoon a few miles from camp. We climbed the rocks and cliffs, the ominous sounds of a thunderstorm in the distance. Randall shivered, his eyes on the sky, his gapped front teeth finding his bottom lip. We felt his fear surround us like warm shadows and we excitedly pointed out nearby lightning strikes we didn't actually see. We told stories of bears and waited for Randall to cry, and when we reached the top and we thought we had him where we wanted him, he suddenly darted away.

The next thing we saw was shirtless Randall cannon-balling off the edge of the cliff, hanging in air for a moment as if he might fly, as if he would move up above us and look down on us for once. But then he fell, and he fell fast. His body, a ball of pink flesh and orange nylon, smacked the water and we winced and thought of our fathers and slamming screen doors at home, our mothers wringing their hands over kitchen sinks.

As Robby dove into the water after Randall, I thought of the rainy nights we'd taken turns holding him down on the floor of our cabin. How we'd swung pillows at him. Some of us stuffing the cases with shoes or rocks—things with weight and heft our arms didn't have. And maybe we'd have stopped if Randall had just said something, done something, but he just took it and so we kept on swinging.

Later, our arms sore and our minds empty, we'd shake off the sound of his stuttered breaths from the bathroom and pretend it didn't feel like they were right near our ears. We'd laugh and climb into our beds and tell each other with our eyes that he was asking for it, being the way he was.

At the top of the cliff, we watched Robby struggle to pull Randall to the shore. Even from far away, we could see Randall's arms and legs fighting the water. His strokes were clumsy and frantic, desperate to stay above the surface. But he was broken and shattered in ways we had always seen. And we felt ourselves crack and pull just a little bit free from him and from everything he was that we hoped like hell we'd never be.

Randall's body eventually collapsed on the edge of the water, his smooth white back pulsing up and down. The silence settled down on all of us and we thought again of our fathers, their stubbled cheeks smiling, their heavy calloused hands landing on the backs of our necks and staying there, warm and weighing us down just like we needed, to keep us from slipping away.

Summer's End

I wasn't supposed to know where my brother snuck off to in the night. I was only supposed to cover for him if Mom or Dad woke up while he was gone. The weight of this responsibility was constricting and inviting—a secret shared between Patrick and me. I never considered what I might tell them if they awoke, but I knew that Patrick trusted me, and for that, I trusted myself.

I knew her name was Miranda. I'd seen Patrick writing it in the steam on the bathroom mirror. I knew she was beautiful because I had peeked at them when they met in the night. She was always dressed in flowing skirts in hundreds of colors; the material was see-through and showed the bikini bottoms she wore underneath. Tied at her waist, she wore a pinstriped button-down that I recognized as belonging to my father. Her long, curly hair was the color of sunset and sand, and it danced with the wind like flames. Her wrists and ankles were covered in bracelets, and every move she made was musical. She held a long white cigarette in her fingers, twirling it like a tiny baton in between smooth, elegant breaths. She would wait for Patrick out near the water. He would run to her from our back deck. The only noise in the night was the crash of the waves and the tinkle of her bracelets on the wind.

I would watch them embrace, then I would creep quietly back to my bedroom, envisioning them on the beach—her dancing and singing poetry while my brother strummed the guitar he'd never really learned how to play. Her jewelry would jingle accompaniment and she would stop only to shower my brother's face with kisses. After seeing her, I understood why he snuck away from our beach house each night. Our parents would never understand Miranda the way we did.

Each morning at sunrise, Patrick would sneak back into the house. I would wake to him sitting on the edge of my bed. Sometimes, if I knew he was there, I would keep my eyes closed just a little longer, breathing in the sweet smoky smell of him, pretending that someone needed me like he needed Miranda. When I opened my eyes, he would search my face and whisper, "All clear?"

I'd give him a thumbs up and watch his body relax into the fatigue he'd been hiding all night. He'd tuck the sheets around me, kiss my head, and slip from the room, returning to his own bed down the hall. In his wake was left a bit of sadness. I wanted him to nestle in next to me like when I was a little girl, telling jokes and tickling my feet. But, I was too old for that and both of us knew it.

Near the end of summer, Patrick shook me awake in the night.

"Get your sweater and sandals. We're going for a walk on the beach."

I raced on tiptoes for the back door. Miranda was waiting for us out in the sand. She waved and ran toward us, her bracelets clinking in the night wind. Her skirt buoyed on the wind; for a moment, she was running on air. She swept me up in her long, brown arms and kissed me on the cheek. The smell of her stayed on my skin; it was sultry and strong and reminded me of the heat of the sun on the back of my neck.

"Oh, Patrick, you brought her! Let's pretend she's ours—just for tonight."

I looked at the dreamy grin spread across Patrick's face. I was a part of his secret world now, and I never wanted to go back home. My brother lit a cigarette from the end of hers, and they both watched me for a moment. The cigarette at his mouth, Patrick looked older and more like our father than ever before. The distinction stretched out between us and I suddenly worried he would scold me or send me back inside.

That night was different from what I had imagined. Patrick hadn't brought his guitar and Miranda didn't sing. They built a fire in the sand, and they smoked and drank cans of beer from a little red cooler. She rolled cigarettes in colorful papers, and when they smoked them, the smell was sweet, almost like Grandpa's cigars. She laughed while blowing the smoke into my face, and I felt my cheeks flush. Her laughter was like wind chimes, and I closed my eyes to see them. They were round and crystal and strung from gold chains. The wind and the sun in my mind created rainbows beneath my eyelids.

I stretched out on the sand by the fire while they ran to the water, stripping as they dove into the waves. As I drifted off to sleep, I thought how cold the water must be, but I didn't say a word—I might break the spell.

I woke to the sunrise and knew we had to go home soon. Patrick sat nearby, staring at the water. Miranda's curly head rested on his lap. Patrick began twirling a piece of her hair in his fingers and smiled down at her sleeping face. When he noticed me watching, I raised my eyebrows, knowing we were short on time. But he just shrugged. He lifted his thumb up and whispered, "All clear." But he was telling me, not asking me, this time.

***

That night was the last time I ever saw Miranda. That was the last summer that our family would spend at the beach house together. That was the last summer that Patrick would live with us. But I didn't know any of that then. All I knew was that the sun was sitting on the edge of the water, and the sand in the wind was blowing through my hair. The air that morning was wonderful and salty and strange; I let it fill my lungs until they ached, and I knew I had to let it out. No air would ever taste that way again.

Taxidermy

My father collects dead animals in the same way a person collects coins. He searches for them, gathers them, catalogs them, and preserves them—never once realizing that no one but another collector would be impressed.

The stuffing of animals began as a vague interest, then developed into a hobby, and at some point, our house became filled with animals of all shapes and sizes staring into the stale air of each room.

The Guinea pig atop our television, its long not-quite-yellow-but-not-quite-white fur lifting in the occasional breeze of an open window.

The gray alley cat near the foot of the stairs, always seeming to have just blinked its narrowed yellow eyes.

The front half of a deer leaned against my mother's old sewing machine, casting shadows in the paths of dust. The deer so lifelike—save the fact that the back half of its body is gone. *Not everything you find is going to be intact,* my father says.

Now that he no longer works, he seems to spend his days moving the animals into new places. When I get home from school, it's like the furniture's been moved and I have to reorient myself to the new lay of the land.

He'll have tucked a small dog into the bed in the guest room and drawn the shades down tight.

He'll pose a sleek red fox in the bathtub, its head angled as if it's drinking from the tap.

Tiny birds of different colors will line the windowsill in the kitchen, poised toward the glass as if ready for flight.

In the night, I have heard my father weeping in this house filled with eyes that cannot see. I have seen him stroking the starchy fur of one of his collection in the dark, as he gasps for air and rocks like a pendulum back and forth. And I think back to the way he silently closed the lid on my mother's casket, his face blank and empty as if in that single moment he had forgotten how to speak or how to feel.

In the Front Room, In the Kitchen

In the front room of the house, the sheet they have placed over the mirror on the mantel has pulled loose. It hangs down just enough so that a strip of afternoon sun disturbs the shadows lurking in the corner of the room. Near another dusty corner, half-empty pill bottles still clutter a basket.

Along one wall, straight-backed chairs remain at attention. The cushions are pale blue leather, smooth like an unblemished egg. In those chairs, the family sat for seven days while friends and family filed through.

A year ago, this floor was covered with a tapestry rug, a swirling pattern of purples, blues, and gray. The children, when they had been small, found shapes and animals and faces in the colors of that rug—the way most kids did with clouds in the sky. To one side, a baby grand piano had once sat, but after the accident, they had to make room for the bed with the metal railing and back that lifted up and down with the press of a button.

Because the rug has not found its way back into the room, ruts show in the wooden floor. Ruts from the wheelchair, from the rolling bed, from the machines, machines, machines. Deeply gashed wheel tracks travel toward the doorsill, leading out to where the sun shines more freely. Where it's not held back by heavy curtains.

Near the front door, the staircase sits silent. Family photographs line the wall along the stairs, many hanging crooked from rubbed shoulders and stomping feet. Near the bottom, is a wedding portrait: white lace, gray tux, roses the pink of a newborn's cheeks. Up the stairs, the family grows—three people, then four, then five. Then, the pictures stop several steps away from the second floor.

Down the hall from the stairs is the kitchen. There, yellow gingham curtains hang limp over the sink. The air in the room is stale. The floor is etched with layers of footprints. Stacks of mail are piled on the table. Dishes and cups and mugs and silverware clutter the counter; some are dirty, most are clean, but none of them has found its way back into place in the cabinets and drawers.

In the kitchen are more family pictures. Not like the formal portraits by the stairs, with their combed hair and pressed clothes. These are snapshots of life pinned haphazardly to a corkboard over the breakfast nook. The parents holding hands at the top of the Empire State Building on their twentieth anniversary. Neither is looking at the camera, only at each other. The older son in marching band, his tuba hugging his tall, slender body. The feather in his uniform cap jaunts to the side, mirroring his crooked smile. The daughter in a silvery leotard with smoothed back hair. She scowls at whoever is taking the picture, but poses just the same. Her pale limbs stretch out beyond the picture's edge.

But the photo of the younger son is torn at the corners where it's been taken down and pinned back up. In it, he's riding his motorbike, sailing through the air over a dirt track. The family has all looked at it, knowing that he is flying there against the sharp blue sky, as if he gives no thoughts to ever coming back down.

Snow in Florida

Five days after Christmas the year I was 11, my mother and I took our first and last road trip together. Just hours earlier, she'd taken the lights off the tree. She sent me up the stepladder to get the star, and then she gently wrapped it in tissue paper and nestled it into a box with all three stockings. And for the fourth day in a row, she said, "I bet your father'll be back in the morning."

I helped her take the decoration boxes up to the attic, and when we climbed back down into the air conditioning, dust clung to our sweaty skin.

Christmas in Florida isn't like Christmas anywhere else.

That's something my dad always said. I never knew if he meant it was better here or worse.

Later, on the couch, she and I watched *Prancer*, the sound of the characters' boots crunching on snow echoed through the room. I watched the little girl's breath make fog in the air as she screamed at her father not to shoot the reindeer, even though he was hurt.

Without turning to look at me, my mother said, "I remember snow like that." And I wondered if she'd talk about when I was a baby, when we'd lived with my grandparents up north, waiting for my father to return. Always waiting for him.

"Do you remember your father insisting we all make snow angels? We took turns holding you. Then, together, we put you in the snow and moved your arms and legs for you. A baby snow angel right between ours."

Of course I didn't remember. But I nodded like I did.

"I want to make snow angels again," she said with a sigh. "Don't you?"

And so at 10:30 at night on the Monday after Christmas, I found myself climbing into the passenger seat of my mother's car.

"We'll just keep driving north," she said. "There's bound to be snow eventually."

I didn't know where she planned on going. My grandparents were dead, the farmhouse auctioned, and we'd moved to where my father was, where palm trees stretched toward sunny skies and nobody seemed to own knitted hats or gloves.

***

When I woke up later, the car was no longer moving. The windows were up, the radio was off, and the car was flooded with light. We were in a truck stop parking lot, the concrete an endless gray blanket in every direction.

Mom was staring straight ahead, still as can be. If it weren't for her wide-open eyes, I'd have thought she was asleep. I cleared my throat and watched her startle. She turned to me and spread her lips into a glass smile.

"Well, hello, sleepyhead. Hungry?"

It was the middle of the night and I just wanted a bed, but I nodded anyway.

***

After the waitress settled plates of pancakes in front of us, I asked, "How much farther do we go?"

"Not much, I think."

She slid her hands across the sticky tabletop toward me. But when I didn't reach back, she pulled them away. She leaned back in the booth and began twisting the thin gold band on her left ring finger, something I knew she did when she was thinking things she didn't want to think.

She excused herself to the restroom, but when I finished eating, she still wasn't back. I found her in a narrow hallway, smiling and laughing with the largest man I'd ever seen. He was so big and so tall, I thought of how he could have taken the star off our tree without a ladder. He wore a puffy blue vest and a stocking cap; thick black gloves dangled from a clip on his belt. I imagined him lying in field of white snow, his arms and legs moving up and down while my mother laughed next to him. I couldn't picture myself in the middle. I wondered how far we were from home.

"You ready, Mom?" I asked, my voice firmer than I felt.

My mother was still facing the man, but she fluttered her eyes in my direction without moving her head. She pulled the car keys from her pocket and said she'd catch up in a minute.

***

Later, after my mother filled the gas tank, she slid into the driver's seat and started the engine. The car turned over on the first try this time.

We pulled to the exit, the highway stretching out before us in two different directions.

"Which way should we go? Home or north?" she asked.

And I stared at her, waiting for her to look at me, but she didn't.

"Tell me about snow angels," I said. "What are they like?"

"What? Now?"

I didn't move, didn't say a word.

She sighed and settled her hands in her lap, turning and turning her ring.

"Well … the snow is cold and wet. But you don't notice it at first when you lie down. You see the white all around you and maybe a little flake of white will land on your eyelash or your finger, and you have to remind yourself how cold it must be. But then you move your arms and legs, shoving the snow and leaving your mark. And the cold slides into you a little, but then your skin melts it, and it's almost like it was never there."

"Should we even bother?" I asked. "It's just going to melt and disappear."

My mother looked at me, finally, and narrowed her eyes. Not like she was angry, but like she was choosing which version of the truth to say.

"That's what makes it so special," she said, turning the car for the moment toward home. "Don't you see?"

Neighborhood Pool Party

Hanging the piñata over the swimming pool was Ned's idea. Lucinda just shrugged her shoulders and shook her head. She'd long ago given up trying to change Ned's mind.

The Hallorans' boy was up first. He swam to the center of the pool, slid on a mask, and swung the stick—nowhere near the target. The excitement quieted as everyone realized the impossibility of breaking a piñata while treading water.

Ned noticed the Sachs' preschooler at the edge of the pool. His trunks were at his ankles, and he was peeing a silent arc directly into the water. Ned caught Lucinda's eye just as she grabbed a bottle of wine and headed into the house.

Grace Biswanger from next door slid beside him, her voice warm on his neck. "My diamond necklace. I lost it in the pool. Can you help me, Neddie?" Her hand trailed down his arm, so gentle it was barely touching his skin.

"I'll see what I can do." Neddy smiled, his eighth cocktail wet in his hand.

When the piñata finally broke, the children swarmed the water. Candy dissolved into rainbow trails. The pool filters choked on floating whistles and yo-yos.

But Ned had already slipped into the quiet darkness beneath the oak tree on the other side of the fence.

Later, after the pool had to be emptied and drained, colorful wrappers and bits of paper surrounded the grates, clumped in piled clusters like dirty confetti.

Ned stood near the edge, gazing at the streaks of plastic and paper, considering the line drawn between having fun and making a mess.

Something shiny caught his eye and he leaned over, too far. As the bottom of the pool hurtled toward him, his final thought was of Mrs. Biswanger's diamond necklace. The one he couldn't remember ever seeing her wear.

Where Nobody Might See

My mother is decorating a birthday cake for my cousin. Bending over our kitchen table, she clutches the white pastry bag that crinkles with each squeeze. Her tongue edges out between her lips as she forms tiny sugar stars and turns the plate. I lean close to watch, blowing my bangs out of my eyes. The screen door slaps as my father comes in and out, loading beer in the car. The sound makes me jump, and one of my braids flops near the cake. My mother sighs, her eyes shifting from the cake to my hair to the back door; her line of vision is strung across the room so tight you could touch it.

On the way to my uncle's house, the red cooler is wedged in the backseat where my feet are supposed to be. I hold my hands and feet against the icy plastic as long as I can bear and then I twist in my seat to shove them on my brother. He laughs and pushes me away, his hands like fire against my frosty skin. The wind blows through the windows, stinging with the smell of cut grass.

Mom's holding the cake on her lap up front. She fusses over turns and railroad tracks, afraid the frosting will smudge. A ruined cake would be just another reason for everyone to remember that she's not from here, that this is Dad's family, not hers.

We spill out of the car and into the house, Mom muttering, "watch it!" between clenched teeth. My brother bursts into the game room where our cousins always are. All boys, their welcome is violent in its joy, hands slapping hands like stuttered applause. I freeze my smile across my face, just like I've seen Mom do a million times, but they greet me with eyes like paper cuts and turn back to the air hockey table that's always broken. My brother takes his place with them and even though the room has no door, I feel the space closed off to me once again.

Without looking, I know that my aunts and uncles have gathered out back where all the coolers are. I can picture the sweaty beer cans in rigid fists, cigarettes dangling from mouths. Through an open window, I hear my mom's laughter cut the air outside. Even her laugh has an accent. Her voice is like a stranger following her from room to room, making other people stop and look and listen. She doesn't drink or smoke and I try to picture where she's putting her hands. Will she arrange her arms across her chest or grab at my father's hand every time he walks away?

I make my way to the kitchen, which is quieter, less smoky, but it smells like onions and old cheese. I sit in one of the yellow chairs, feeling it stick to my thighs. I rub my fingers across the tears in the plastic where soft cotton pokes through and think of our own fabric chairs at home. I drag my foot across the threadbare kitchen carpet, the color of rust with yellow and green circles the same size as my big toe, considering the chipped nail polish that my mother's been telling me to remove for at least a week. I wonder how long before someone will find their way into the kitchen and if they'll even notice I'm there. I imagine my mother and me sitting at the table together, our smooth smiles and her laughter filling the room.

Someone has taken the plastic wrap off the cake where it sits on the table next to my mother's cake knife and a stack of small paper plates waiting to be filled. I lightly touch where the frosting has hardened, not a single smudge in sight. Before I can stop myself, I dig my fingers in and swipe a row of blue and yellow stars near the back where I think nobody might see. I stuff my sugar laden fingers into my mouth, and the sweetness makes my throat want to close. Then I sit on my sticky, stained hands and wait for someone to come into the room and try to make me move.

Block Party Games

With special permission from the homeowners' association, wooden barricades were set up at either end of the block. The white and orange diagonal stripes created our own little hazard zone.

Balloons strung from mailboxes bounced in the late morning breeze. Picnic tables were set up near the cul-de-sac jutting off our block, where the bigger, better houses were. The plastic tablecloths lifted and fell as the DJ, Mr. Ryker from across the street, played Top 40 hits at a card table flanked by two enormous black speakers. Across from him, a bounce house shuddered as little kids catapulted inside against the red and yellow nylon.

We arrived late and nobody acted surprised. As we crossed the street, Dad draped his arm around Mom's shoulders, grasping the upper arm of the sweater he insisted she wear. We piled our plates with pasta salad, watermelon, and hot dogs. I sidled up to the dessert table, but Mom wrinkled her nose, her eyes falling to the slope of my 12-year-old stomach.

Dad started toward a table away from the rest, but Mom stopped him. *Steve. Over here. They'll make room.* And people did.

Mom hung her sweater across the back of her chair. *It's so hot out here.* Her voice to no one and everyone at the same time. Dad turned away.

After lunch, the games would begin. An egg toss. A three-legged race. A shoe scramble. In past years, we always sat out. But Dad had decided we should play this year. Another on the long list of changes he was trying to make.

We didn't see the Valkyries arrive, but it made sense that they were there. The tables were set up near the end of their driveway after all. I caught Mr. Valkyrie eyeing us and knew they had thought just like us. *They won't show up this year.* But we were all there. Smiling and laughing and waiting to see what would happen next.

And that's when Mrs. Valkyrie threw an egg at my mother.

Dad and Mom partnered for the egg toss while I sat on the curb, shoving brownies into my mouth. About eight rounds in, I heard a shriek. Mom stood there, her own egg caught in her fist but the Valkyries' egg was dripping from her head. A red welt flowered on her forehead where it had hit.

Mom lurched toward Mrs. Valkyrie.

Mr. Valkyrie stepped in front of his wife.

And Dad just stood, waiting for his egg to be thrown back, like the game wasn't over.

Mrs. Valkyrie spewed a stream of horrible names at my mother, words I wouldn't have thought Mrs. Valkyrie knew, and Dad pivoted toward her. As he approached, I thought he might scoop her into his arms, kiss her, show Mr. Valkyrie things could go both ways. But he pushed past her and kept going. His legs rushing him past the bounce house and beyond, toward where the houses grew smaller and the yards were more dirt than grass.

I stood and brushed the crumbs from my lap. Mom came at me, clutching thick green rope in her hands. The egg had started to harden into crusted streaks in her hair, and as she leaned over to tie my leg to hers, I touched her hair to see if it still felt wet.

When I pulled my hand away, she looped her arm with mine and, together on our three legs, we staggered back to our house, the pulpy sound of the speakers filling the air behind us.

Dollhouse

From her mattress on the floor, the girl tries to block out the noise from downstairs, the music, the glass breaking, the laughter too loud for anything to have been funny. The sounds that sometimes push past the lock of her bedroom door and the dresser she pushes against it; the sounds that hunt for her in the tangle of blankets that used to swallow her whole.

But as the night grows darker, the girl turns out her lights, unfolds herself, and climbs into the small wooden house in the corner of her room.

She slides aside the tiny staircase and the miniature couch with matching side chairs. She stacks the end tables on top of each other and balances them atop the coffee table. She moves the beds to one side, careful not to disturb the family that lays under handkerchief blankets, each member touching another. And she pulls her legs underneath her, curves her back to the slope of the roof, stretching into the pinches of what might no longer fit.

She runs her hands over her skin, bloomed with delicate hives, finding intricate patterns in her scabs. She feels the gentle teeth of the bugs in her unwashed hair, waiting for them to settle into the crevices behind her ears, imagining it's their voices that echo in her head.

As she tucks her chin to her chest, she waits for morning, when the darkness will bend and break, letting in the cool light of day. And she will pull her fingers free from the grate of the tiny windows and dig her toes into the soft wood of the house's floors. She will touch the family's impossibly tiny smiles and wish herself smaller to be a part of their world.

Denise Howard Long's short fiction has appeared in *Pank, Smokelong Quarterly, Pithead Chapel, The Tishman Review, The Evansville Review, Blue Monday Review*, and elsewhere. Her story "What We See" was selected for inclusion in *Best Small Fictions 2018*. She's been awarded residencies at Hedgebrook and Dorland Mountain Arts Colony. Her short story "Recuerdos Olvidados" was runner-up for the Larry Brown Short Story Award, and her story "Where It's Buried" won *Five on the Fifth's* Annual Short Story Contest. Originally from Illinois, Denise currently lives in Nebraska, with her husband and two sons. You can visit her online at www.denisehlong.com.